Where Are You Going, Little Mouse?

by **Robert Kraus**

pictures by **Jose Aruego**
and **Ariane Dewey**

A MULBERRY PAPERBACK BOOK  New York

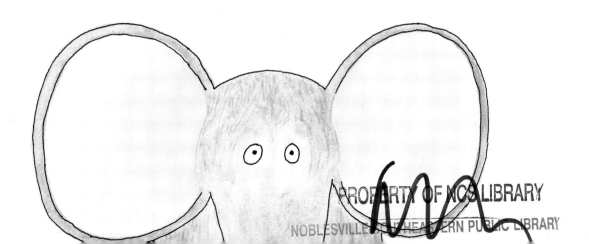

The artwork was prepared as black pen-and-ink
line drawings which were combined with full-color
paintings. The typeface is Avant Garde Gothic.

Library of Congress Cataloging in Publication Data

Kraus, Robert, (date)
Where are you going, little mouse?
Summary: A little mouse runs away from home to find
a "nicer" family, but when darkness comes, he misses
them and realizes how much he loves them.
1. Children's stories, American. [1. Mice—Fiction.
2. Runaways—Fiction]   I. Aruego, Jose, ill.
II. Dewey, Ariane, ill.   III. Title.
PZ7.K868Wh 1985   [E]   84-25868
ISBN 0-688-08747-7

For Bruce,
Billy,
Pamela,
Mary Anne,
and
Parker
—R. K.

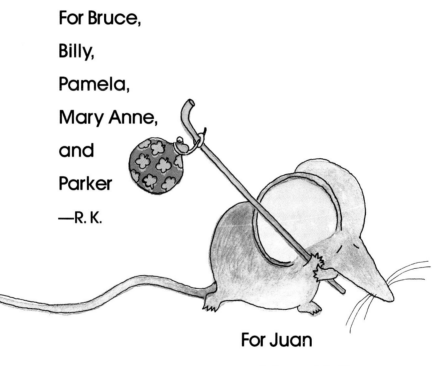

For Juan
—J. A. and A. D.

Where are you going, little mouse?

As far from home as I can go.

What of your mother?
What of your father?

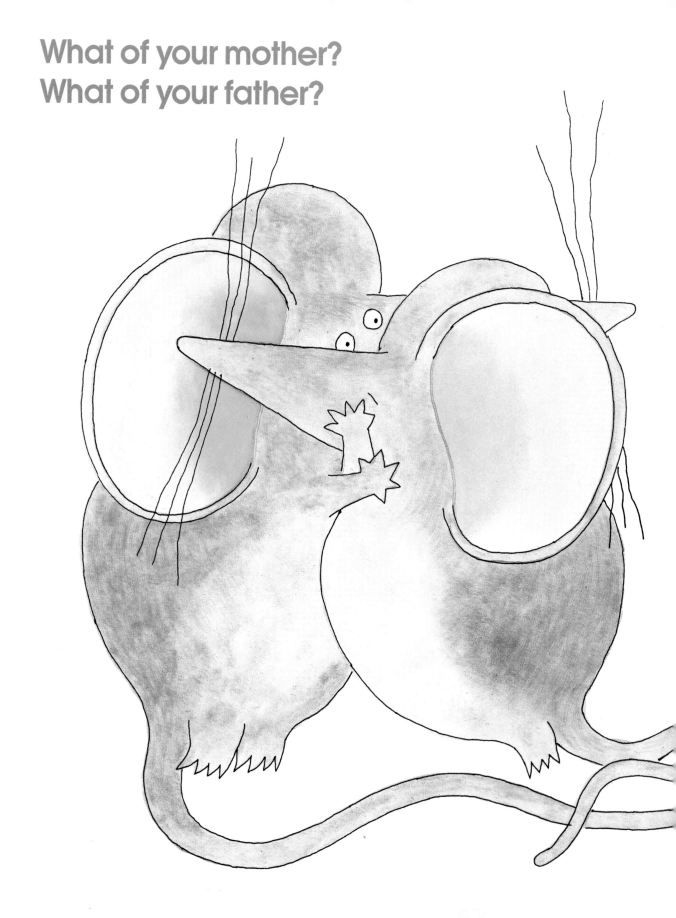

They don't love me.
They won't miss me.

What will you do?

Find a new father who plays with me.

Find a new mother who stays with me.

Find a new brother who isn't mean.

**Find a new sister.
We're a team.**

I'm still looking…
I miss my mother.

I'm exploring...
I miss my father.

I'm still searching…
I miss my sister.

I'm still trying...
I miss my brother.

It's getting dark.
What will you do?

Make a phone call.

Mother, Father,
please don't worry.
Come and get me.
Hurry, hurry.

By the way
they kiss and hug me,
I can tell
they really love me.
I love them, too.

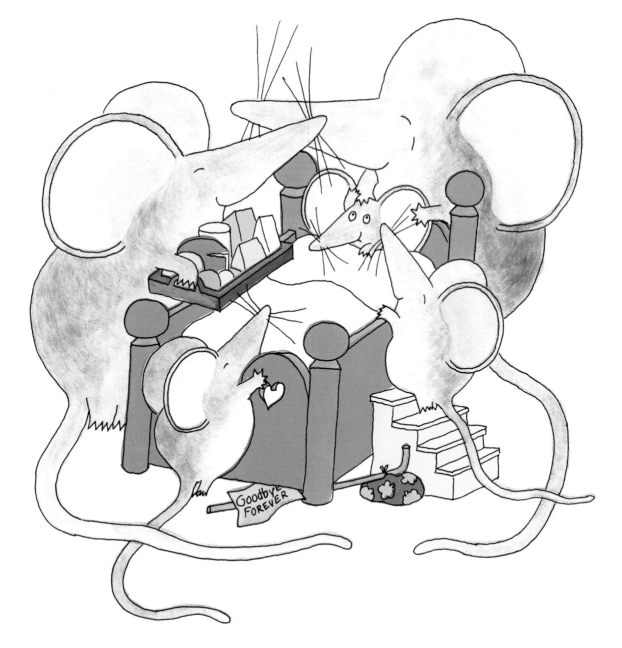